east central regional library

This item was purchased with money from Minnesota's Arts and Cultural Heritage Fund.

CLEAN
WATER
LAND &
LEGACY
AMENDMENT

MINNESOTA
LIBRARY LEGACY

*To my children, Mary, Elizabeth, and Michael,
who were such a good audience forty years ago,
and to my wife, Lynne, who has patiently endured
my silliness over the years.*

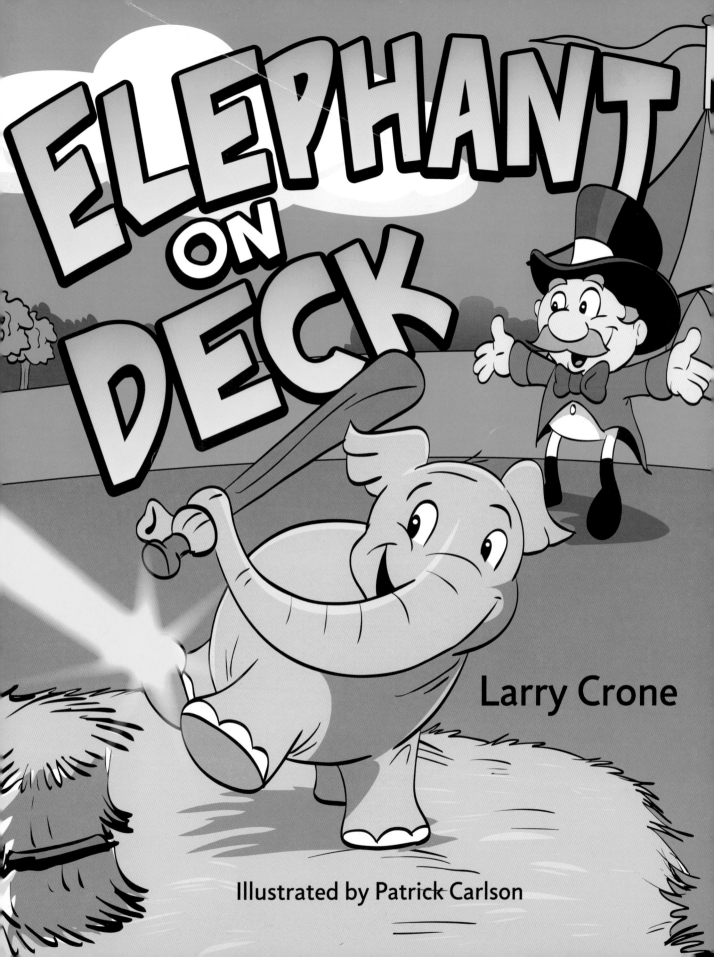

Once there was a baby elephant named Humphrey. He lived with his mother and father, some other elephants, and an elephant trainer. They were part of a circus that traveled from town to town, putting on shows for people who lived nearby.

Humphrey was happy when they came to a new town, because he loved the circus parade. The elephants would walk in a row, each elephant's trunk holding the tail of the elephant in front. Humphrey always came last, his trunk just barely reaching up to his mother's tail. People always pointed at him, clapping and cheering.

But Humphrey was not happy very often. Usually, he was bored and lonely. When the other elephants practiced for the show, he could only watch. And when they performed in the big tent, he couldn't even do that! Hearing the "ooh's" and "aah's" only made him sadder and more lonely.

Sometimes, he would watch children playing off in the distance. They seemed to be having a lot of fun. He was especially interested when they played baseball. He would see them throw the ball, swing the bat, and run around cheering and yelling.

One day when he was especially lonely, he decided he would go and play with the children. As he walked across the field, he found some clumps of tall grass which looked tasty. He used his trunk to pull up a clump of grass, roots and all. Then he gave it a shake so most of the dirt fell off, and ate the rest. That may not sound very pleasant, but elephants do not mind a little dirt with their grass. In fact, the fresh grass tasted so good compared to the hay he usually ate, that he looked for more nice clumps as he walked across the field.

Soon, he was surprised to find that he had crossed the field, but the children were not there anymore. What should he do? Beyond the field were some woods. He had never been in a place like that. It looked dark and crowded and it made him nervous. But he wanted to find the children, so he went into the woods.

After just a few steps Humphrey heard a loud, "PEE WEE." He was trying to decide if he should be afraid when he saw a little bird sitting on a high branch. It opened its tiny beak and said, "PEE WEE." He confidently walked a little farther and saw another little bird hopping around in the bushes. This bird said, "TEA-cher, TEA-cher, TEA-cher..." over and over. This little bird was even louder than the first one! He was so impressed that such little birds could make so much noise that without thinking about it he pulled down a branch with his trunk and stripped off the leaves. *My, that tasted good!* he thought. After wandering for a while, tasting different leaves, and listening to the sounds, he realized that he was lost.

With all the trees around, he couldn't see the circus or even the field he had crossed! Now he was afraid and lonelier than he had ever been. He tried going one direction, and then another, but only got more confused.

Then he heard a faint but familiar sound. It was the sound of children playing off in the distance. It cheered him up to think that he would find them after all. He started to follow the sound and gradually it grew louder.

Eventually he came to the edge of the woods, and there they were, playing baseball! He had come out of the woods at a different place. The circus was nowhere to be seen, but he didn't let that bother him.

For a while, he just watched them play. He had never been this close to a baseball game before. Then a boy hit the ball and everybody started running and yelling. Humphrey got so excited that he started running and yelling too. The children had not seen him at first, but elephants yell very loudly. The children all stopped and looked at him. Baby elephants are not really very small. And when one is running, waving its trunk, and yelling, it looks very big! The children ran away as fast as they could.

When Humphrey got to where they had dropped the bat, he picked it up and discovered that he could swing it pretty well. The children had been afraid, but they were even more curious. They thought, *Is that really an elephant running out of the woods?* As soon as they realized that Humphrey wasn't chasing them, they peeked out from behind the trees to see what would happen next.

When they saw him swinging the bat, a little boy said, "I think he wants to play!" They slowly came back to the field, and another boy picked up the ball and threw it to Humphrey.

Humphrey was finally going to play baseball! He swung the bat, but didn't come close to hitting the ball. That was a disappointment, but he thought he might do better if he got another chance. Somebody picked up the ball and threw it back to the pitcher. Humphrey's second swing was no better than his first. He didn't hit the ball on his third, fourth, or fifth try, either.

The children were excited. They were playing baseball with an elephant! They were laughing and joking with each other. But Humphrey was getting more and more discouraged. He thought the children were laughing at him because he was such a bad player. After a few more misses, he gave up. He had wanted to play baseball so badly, but he couldn't do it no matter how hard he tried.

He didn't know how to get back to the circus and he really didn't care. He dropped the bat and just started walking away, dragging his trunk on the ground. He was too little to be in one of the circus acts, and he couldn't play baseball. He didn't have any idea what to do. So he just kept on walking.

He was walking along a narrow road, and a big truck passed him. After the driver got over his surprise, he called the police and said, "There's a little elephant walking along the road over here."

The policeman called the circus and asked, "Are you missing an elephant?" Before long, one of the circus trucks stopped beside him. The elephant trainer got out, opened the door, and Humphrey followed him into the back of the truck. When they got back to the circus, his mother and father and the other elephants fussed over him, but it didn't cheer him up. His trunk was still dragging on the ground.

The next day, he just sniffed at the hay that the elephant trainer brought him. He had nothing to look forward to. That afternoon, the trainer came and said, "Some children told me you were playing baseball with them."

Humphrey thought, *And they laughed at me!*

The trainer said, "I want you to try something for me. It's really hard to hit a baseball, but I have a bat and a ball that should make it easier." He held out a fat plastic bat in one hand and in the other a beach ball almost as big as Humphrey 's head. "Here, take this bat and try to hit the ball." Humphrey took the bat in his trunk, and when the trainer tossed the ball to him, he swung the bat and missed, of course. But the trainer insisted that he try again.

The trainer tossed the ball. Humphrey swung the bat, and he hit the ball! Not very hard, and not very far, but he hit it! After that he was eager to practice more and was soon hitting the ball as often as he missed. Sometimes he hit it just right and it would sail over the trainer's head.

Humphrey was having fun and almost couldn't believe his ears when the trainer said, "I think this will make a really good act for the show if we practice enough." Humphrey was so happy! He was going to get to play baseball, and he was going to have an act in the circus! He was so very, very happy that his trunk didn't come near the ground for a long, long time.

The End

Note to the reader:

Many years ago, probably in a spontaneous effort to provide my wife with a few minutes relief from mothering, I announced to my three young children that I would tell them the story of The Elephant in the Pantry. Whatever muse was on call that day never got the elephant into the pantry, but did inspire a story the kids wanted to hear again and again. The inappropriate name stuck and became something of a joke. I am hoping my children will forgive me for changing it to a more appropriate one for this printing.

Have a book idea?

Contact us at:

Mascot Books
560 Herndon Parkway
Suite 120
Herndon, VA 20170

info@mascotbooks.com | www.mascotbooks.com